Weekly Reader Presents

Sprocket, Dog Detective

(Original Title: Follow That Fraggle!)

By Louise Gikow

Pictures by Barbara Lanza

Muppet Press

Holt, Rinehart and Winston

NEW YORK

Published by Holt, Rinehart and Winston,
383 Madison Avenue, New York, New York 10017.

Library of Congress Cataloging in Publication Data
Gikow, Louise.
Follow that Fraggle!
Summary: Sprocket the dog has an exciting day when
he follows Uncle Traveling Matt Fraggle, the famous
Fraggle explorer.
1. Children's stories, American.   [1. Puppets—
Fiction.   2. Dogs—Fiction]   I. Lanza, Barbara, ill.
II. Title.
PZ7.G369Fo   1985   [E]   85-5479
ISBN: 0-03-004558-4

First Edition
Printed in the United States of America
1 3 5 7 9 10 8 6 4 2

ISBN 0-03-004558-4

This book is a presentation of
Weekly Reader Books

Weekly Reader Books offers book clubs for children
from preschool through junior high school.

For further information write to:
Weekly Reader Books
4343 Equity Drive
Columbus, Ohio 43228

Sprocket, Dog Detective

SOMEWHERE in a town a lot like yours lives an inventor named Doc and his dog, Sprocket.

In Doc's workshop, there is a little hole in the wall. And through that hole is a very special place called Fraggle Rock.

Doc doesn't know anything about the Fraggles. He's never seen one. But his dog, Sprocket, has seen a Fraggle or two in his time. Sprocket doesn't know what Fraggles are, but he thinks they are *very* interesting.

Doc keeps very busy doing one thing or another. Often, he goes out and leaves Sprocket alone in the workshop. When Doc isn't home, Sprocket doesn't have much to do except roll a ball around or chew on an old bone.

One day, Sprocket was lying in his basket, feeling as bored as a dog can feel, when he heard a noise. *Maybe Doc is home early!* Sprocket thought happily.

But it wasn't Doc at all. It was a Fraggle!

The Fraggle looked like he was dressed for a long journey. He was wearing hiking boots and carrying a walking stick, and he had a pack on his back.

What Sprocket didn't know was that he was Uncle Traveling Matt Fraggle—the famous Fraggle explorer!

What Sprocket *did* know was that he wasn't feeling quite as bored as he had been before.

Traveling Matt tiptoed to the door. He was trying to avoid
Sprocket. You see, Traveling Matt thought of Sprocket as a
huge, hairy, possibly dangerous Beast who might want to eat
him. Sprocket, on the other hand, thought of Traveling
Matt as a small, fuzzy, interesting creature who might be fun
to play with.

I wonder where he's going, Sprocket thought. Maybe . . .
I'll follow him and find out!

So when Traveling Matt stepped through the dog door
and out of Doc's workshop, Sprocket was hot on the trail!

Sprocket followed Traveling Matt down the street. This wasn't hard, because Traveling Matt had short legs and walked pretty slowly.

First Traveling Matt stopped at a fire hydrant. He tipped his hat to the hydrant and said something Sprocket couldn't hear. Then he seemed to listen while the fire hydrant said something back!

Hmmm, thought Sprocket. *That's strange. I've visited a lot of hydrants in my time, but none of them ever talked to* me.

Then Traveling Matt went into a movie theater. Sprocket
had to sneak in after him, because dogs were *not* allowed.

The movie was about a boy and his dog. It was very exciting.

When the hero of the movie got in trouble, Traveling Matt went to the rescue. "Let me pass!" cried Traveling Matt. "That Silly Creature needs help!"

Sprocket thought this was all very exciting, and lots of fun. "Woof, woof!" he barked. "Woof, woof, woof!"

When the manager of the theater heard Traveling Matt yelling and Sprocket barking, he ran up to the front of the theater and onto the stage. He grabbed Traveling Matt first, and then he picked up Sprocket.

"You two are coming to the office with me," he said angrily. "And then I'm calling the Dog Pound!"

In the manager's office, Sprocket and Traveling Matt looked at each other for a long moment. "Hello, Beast," Traveling Matt finally said. "Since we seem to be sharing a cave for the moment, I suppose we should be on speaking terms. My name is Traveling Matt, and I'm from Fraggle Rock. Who are you?"

"Woof!" barked Sprocket.

"What an interesting name," said Traveling Matt nervously. "You know, Woof, I'm sure you are a simply charming Beast. And it certainly was nice of that Silly Creature to find us a place to live. But I have some more exploring to do, and I really must be on my way."

Traveling Matt pushed on the door. It wouldn't budge, so he tried knocking.

"Excuse me," said Traveling Matt politely when the manager opened the door. "This door seemed to be stuck. Thank you for opening it."

"Hey!" said the manager. "What's going on here? You're not a dog!"

"Sorry," said the manager. "You can take your dog home now. Just make sure he doesn't go to any more movies!"

"What's a dog?" Traveling Matt asked Sprocket as they walked away.

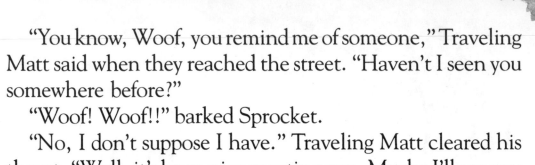

"You know, Woof, you remind me of someone," Traveling Matt said when they reached the street. "Haven't I seen you somewhere before?"

"Woof! Woof!!" barked Sprocket.

"No, I don't suppose I have." Traveling Matt cleared his throat. "Well, it's been nice meeting you. Maybe I'll see you again sometime." And Traveling Matt turned and trotted off into the sunset.

When Sprocket got back home, he was so tired from his
adventure that he lay down for a nap. A few minutes later
Doc walked in.

"Hi, Sprocket!" said Doc.

Sprocket yawned.

"You know," Doc went on, scratching Sprocket in that very special place behind the ears, "it's too bad. I go to work every day and you're stuck here all alone. You didn't have a very exciting day today, did you, boy? How about going for a nice run in the park?"

Sprocket shook his head. Doc would never know just how exciting his day had really been!